CW00859330

Text copyright © 1988 Shirley Isherwood
Illustrations copyright © 1988 Jolyne Knox

First published in Great Britain in 1988
by Macdonald & Co (Publishers) Ltd

Reprinted in 1989 by Macdonald Children's Books

Photoset in 16pt Plantin by Keene Graphics Ltd, London
Colour origination by Scantrans Pte Ltd, Singapore

Printed and bound in Belgium by
Proost International Book Production

Macdonald Children's Books
Simon and Schuster International Group
Wolsey House, Wolsey Road
Hemel Hempstead HP2 4SS

BRITISH LIBRARY CATALOGUING IN PUBLICATION DATA
Isherwood, Shirley
Alice alone.
I. Title II. Knox, Jolyne
823'.914[J]

ISBN 0-356-16520-5
ISBN 0-356-16521-3 Pbk

Shirley Isherwood

ALICE ALONE

Illustrated by Jolyne Knox

Macdonald Children's Books

For
Sarah Louise Himelfield

Chapter One

Alice and Scooter's mother had been ill
with flu. Just as she got better, Father
became ill — and it was then that
Grandpa came to the rescue. He drove to
the house in his old red pick-up truck, and
said that he would take Alice and Scooter
to his farm for a few days.

The farm was small, and high up on
the moors.

Grandpa had lived there ever since he was a small boy. He said that he would never leave it. Even when Grandma died, he wouldn't consider leaving.

He said that towns made him feel as though he was in a prison. He would stay where he was, with his sheep and hens, and where he could see the moors and the sky all around him.

Mrs Hammond came from the village each day, and cleaned the house for him, and cooked his food. It was, said Grandpa, a good arrangement.

Alice thought that going to stay at the farm was a good arrangement. It was winter, and she had never seen the farm in winter-time.

But Alice's mother wasn't so sure about Grandpa's plan. "Will you be able to manage with two children?" she said.

"Of course I'll manage!" said Grandpa — and he went upstairs, to help Alice and Scooter to pack. He bundled everything into the bags — jeans and shirts, sweaters and socks, and Scooter's stuffed toy kangaroo, called Booker.

No one knew
why Scooter loved
Booker so much —
or why he called
him Booker —
for he was old and
battered, and had
lost his squeak and

one ear. But Scooter wouldn't go anywhere
without him.

Scooter's real name was James, but he
ran about so quickly that everyone called
him Scooter. Now, with his bag banging
against his knees, he ran down the path to
the red pick-up truck.

Alice stayed behind for a moment, to say
goodbye to her mother. "It really is a good
arrangement!" she said. Then she ran to
join Scooter and Grandpa.

Chapter Two

Alice and Scooter had been staying at the farm for three days, when it began to snow heavily.

As soon as Alice woke up she knew that it had been snowing, for the white fields and moors cast a dazzling light in her little bedroom. Alice went to the window and looked out. The scene was beautiful, she thought.

But Grandpa, who was up already, had found that one of the ewes was lost somewhere in the snow. She was going to have a lamb, he said, and he must go out at once and find her.

"Look after Scooter," said Grandpa. "And be good. Mrs Hammond will be here very soon."

Alice waved goodbye to him, and watched as he went over the field, leaving a trail of footprints in the snow. Beside Grandpa's footprints were the pawprints of Ned, the dog.

The footprints and the pawprints looked so nice that Alice thought she would like to make some herself. So she got dressed, put on her wellingtons, and went to wake Scooter up.

Scooter was fast asleep under the patchwork quilt of the bed. Alice prodded him with her finger, and he sat up and rubbed his eyes, and looked at her.

"It's been snowing in the night," said Alice, "and one of Grandpa's sheep is lost. She's going to have a lamb!"

Scooter got out of bed, and ran to the
window. "I can't see the lamb!" he said.
"Is it born yet?"

"I don't know," said Alice. "But when it
is, Grandpa will find it and bring it
home."

Scooter came from the window, and sat
down on the edge of the bed. "I'm
hungry!" he said.

"Get dressed and put your wellingtons
on," said Alice, "and we'll make footprints
in the snow like Grandpa's, and have our
breakfast outside."

"Can we?" said Scooter. He put on his jeans and sweater, and thick socks. Then he followed Alice down the stairs, and put on his wellingtons. His anorak hung behind the door, and he put it on and zipped up all the zips. Then he put on his woolly hat, and pulled it down until it almost covered his eyes.

Alice put on her own anorak and hat. Then she took some bread from the bin, and put some butter and honey on it. She gave one slice to Scooter, and took the other slice for herself.

13

"Can we really eat our breakfast outside in the snow?" said Scooter, as Alice opened the door.

"Yes," said Alice. "I did it all the time when I was little."

"*I* did it when I was little too," said Scooter. He didn't like it when Alice said that she had done something he had not.

"No, you didn't," said Alice.

"I *did!*" said Scooter, and he stumped off, angrily, to the bottom of the garden. Alice followed him, and looked out over the low stone wall. All around, the fields were white with snow, and the sky was very grey and low.

"I had my breakfast outside!" said
Scooter. "I did it four years ago!" He
climbed up on to the stone wall, and stood
glaring down at Alice.

"Don't be silly,"
said Alice, "you're
only just five *now*!"

Scooter began to look angry again — so
to take his mind off his age, Alice began to
make footprints.

Scooter came down from the wall, and
he and Alice walked in circles in the deep
snow. The honey from Scooter's bread ran
down his anorak, and his hat slipped
further down over his eyes.

15

When the garden was full of footprints, Alice and Scooter began to make a snowman.

"I'm hungry," said Scooter, when the snowman was almost finished. "I want eggs, and porridge, and toast and tea."

"Mrs Hammond will make it for you when she comes," said Alice.

"When will she come?" asked Scooter.

"Soon," said Alice — but when she looked over the fields, to where the lane led to the village, there was no Mrs Hammond to be seen.

"*I* want my breakfast *now*," said
Scooter.

"I can't make eggs and porridge and
toast," said Alice. "I can only make bread
and honey."

"I'll have bread and honey," said
Scooter. He began to dig in the snow, for
some small stones to make the snowman's
buttons.

"Get it yourself!"
said Alice. She was
making the
snowman's face,
and she didn't
want to stop.

"I can't make
bread and honey,"
said Scooter, still
digging in the
snow.

Alice looked at him. He seemed very small, and his face was dirty — for he had reached the earth beneath the snow, and the honey on his cheeks was mixed with soil. Alice felt filled with love for him.

"I'll make you bread and honey!" she said. "I'll make you lots!"

She brushed the snow from her mittens, and went into the house.

Chapter Three

Grandpa's old dog, Nell, was lying on the rug, and she wagged her tail as Alice came into the kitchen. Alice stood by the table and carefully buttered three slices of bread, and spread them with honey.

When Scooter came into the kitchen, he took the slices in his grubby hand, and sat down beside Nell, to eat. Alice made some more bread and honey for herself.

When Scooter had eaten his bread, he put the curved crusts on the plate. They were just the same shape as a smile. So Alice took a crust and went outside, and stuck it on the snowman's face. When she came back, Nell was eating the last of the crusts.

"She's hungry," said Scooter. "Everyone is hungry. When will Grandpa come back? Where is Mrs Hammond? Why is she late?"

Alice looked at him. He was frowning. Scooter always liked the same things to happen every day, and already he was

20

used to Mrs Hammond arriving at nine o'clock, in her red woolly hat and mittens, and carrying her big shopping bag.

"Where's Mrs Hammond?" he said again — for he also liked his questions to be answered at once.

"The snow's made her late," said Alice. "It takes longer to walk in the snow."

For a moment she saw Scooter's frown deepen, then it faded away. "All the animals are hungry," he said.

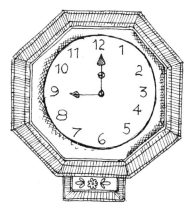

Alice looked at the big clock on the wall. It was gone nine o'clock, and Scooter was right — everyone should have been fed: the two cats, Thomas and Jacob; Kenny the pony; and the hens in their little wooden hen-house.

"There's only me to do it," said Alice. "Well, me and you." But then she looked at Scooter and thought about how little he was. "I have to look after Scooter too," she told herself. "I have to look after the animals and Scooter and myself."

"We have to be good," she said aloud to Scooter. "We have to be very good."

"I *am* being good," said Scooter.

Alice gave Nell some dog biscuits, and the cats some fish that Grandpa had cooked the night before.

She looked carefully amongst the fish, and took out all the small bones, as she had seen Grandpa do, before she put the two bowls on the floor.

"What do hens eat?" she asked Scooter.

"Cakes and trifle and ice-cream," said Scooter. These were his favourite foods.

"Don't be silly," said Alice.

"They do," said Scooter. "They eat ham and jam and legs of lamb." He sat down on the rug, and hugged his knees and laughed at his joke.

"Stop it!" said Alice.

Scooter hunched up over his bent knees, and looked at her. "They eat hen-food," he said. "It's in the cupboard."

Alice opened the cupboard door, and there, as Scooter had said, was a big sack, with the word 'hen-food' written on it. Alice put some in a paper bag, and put on her hat and anorak. Then she took the egg-basket from the hook behind the door.

Scooter put on his hat and anorak, and zipped up his zips again. "My anorak's all sticky," he said. "Why is it sticky?"

24

"You know why," said Alice, as they went out of the back door. "You spilled your honey down it."

"I didn't," said Scooter. "It fell off my bread. On purpose. Why did it do that?"

Alice ignored him, and opened the door of the hen-house.

It was dark inside the hen-house, and smelled of dust and feathers. The hens were sitting on their nests, but when they saw Scooter and Alice they started to flutter about.

Alice put their food in the trough, and
began to collect the eggs. They were warm,
and she laid them carefully, one by one, in
the basket.

Scooter climbed up on a box, and
rubbed the little window clean with his
sleeve. "It's snowing again," he said. "It's
snowing hard."

Alice climbed up behind him, and looked
out. The flakes were very big, and they
blew about in the wind.

Already the footprints in the garden were full of fresh, white snow, and the black stone buttons of the snowman could no longer be seen. The flakes blew against the little window, and lay so thick that Alice and Scooter could scarcely see the house, or the stable that stood in a corner of the field.

Chapter Four

The wind was cold, and the snow blew
against their faces, as Alice and Scooter
made their way across the field. The snow
lay against the front of Scooter's anorak,
and he stopped and brushed it away. Then
he took Booker from his pocket, and began
to push him down between his anorak and
his sweater.

"There's no time for that!" said Alice. "We've got to feed Kenny."

But Scooter stood still in the whirling snow, and soon he had almost disappeared amongst the falling flakes.

"Scooter — come *on!*" shouted Alice.

It seemed a long time before he came to her side — and when at last he did arrive, Alice saw that his head was bare and that he had melting snowflakes in his hair.

"Where's your hat?" she said.

"Booker's got it," said Scooter.

Alice looked at the bulge in front of Scooter's anorak, which was Booker and the woolly hat.

Then quickly, before Scooter could stop
her, she unzipped his anorak, grabbed
the hat by its bobble, and put it back on
his head.

"Booker doesn't need a hat," she said, as
she zipped up his zip again. Then she took
hold of his hand, and together they
struggled the rest of the way over the field,
and went into Kenny's stable.

The pony whinnied when he saw Alice
and Scooter, and his breath made little
clouds of mist in the air. His winter coat

was thick and rough, and Alice laid her
cheek against his side for a moment,
before putting some pony-nuts in the feed
bucket. Alice pulled some hay from a
hay bale, and put it in the manger.

While Kenny ate, Alice and Scooter sat
on the straw bale. Through the open door
they could see the snow falling on the fields
and moor.

"Why hasn't Grandpa come back?"
asked Scooter.

"I don't know," said Alice.

"Perhaps he isn't coming back," said Scooter.

"Of course he is!" said Alice. But suddenly she felt afraid. Suppose Grandpa *didn't* come back? Suppose Mrs Hammond couldn't make her way to the farm house through the snow? Alice and Scooter would be left alone. Alice didn't like to have such frightening thoughts.

"Grandpa's coming back!" she shouted at Scooter. "You're stupid to say that he won't come back!"

Scooter got very angry, and red in the face. "*I'm* not stupid," he said. "*You're* stupid."

Alice stared at him, and he wriggled away from her, and sat at the end of the straw bale. "A wolf has eaten him," he said softly.

"There aren't any wolves," said Alice.

"Yes, there are," said Scooter.

Alice ignored him. To make herself feel better she began to tell herself a little story about how Grandpa would find the lamb, and bring it into the kitchen, to warm it by the stove, and give it a drink of milk.

Grandpa had often told her of how he did this with a lamb that had been born in the snow. "To give it a good start," he said. "Everything needs a good start in life." Perhaps, thought Alice, Grandpa would let her hold the bottle while the lamb sucked.

It was a wonderful thought. But when she looked through the door of the stable again, and gazed out over the moors, she couldn't see Grandpa with the ewe and the lamb. And there was no sign of Mrs Hammond, in her red hat, coming along the lane.

When Kenny had finished eating, Alice and Scooter began to make their way back to the house.

They were just nearing the gate, when Scooter gave a loud cry. Alice turned, and saw him unzipping his anorak.

"Booker's gone!" he said. "The wolf's eaten him!"

"There isn't a wolf," said Alice. "You just imagined it."

"There *is* a wolf," said Scooter, "and he's got Booker!"

Before Alice could stop him, Scooter turned and ran off over the field. Alice ran after him. "Scooter!" she called, "come back here!"

But Scooter was nowhere to be seen. Alice could see nothing but the big, white snowflakes, falling faster and faster. Then, through the flakes, she saw a dark shape, moving towards her on four legs.

"Scooter!" screamed Alice. "It's the wolf! Run!"

Bravely she turned, and shouted, "Go away — go away!"

But the dark shape just came nearer and nearer, making an awful cry. "HOO-HOO!" it said.

Then — "HOO, I'm a wolf!" said Scooter; for it *was* Scooter, Alice could see that now.

Alice took hold of Scooter's hand, and
pulled him along behind her — over the
field, through the garden, and into the
house. She was very angry. "You're
naughty," she said. "Very naughty!"

But Scooter just smiled gently, and stood
in the middle of the kitchen holding
Booker in his hand. "I found him," he
said. "The wolf hadn't eaten him."

Alice looked at him, and stopped feeling
angry. After all, she told herself, he's only
five, and I'm eight.

Chapter Five

Alice and Scooter took off their wet
clothes and put on dry ones and Alice sat
Booker on the top of the stove, to dry. He
was very wet, and the heat of the stove
made a cloud of steam rise from his
battered little body.

The sight made Scooter laugh, and he
rolled about on the rug, snorting and
hiccuping.

"Be quiet!" said Alice. "I'm thinking."

She was picturing in her mind what would happen if neither Grandpa nor Mrs Hammond came. Little by little the fire would die out — for Alice was not allowed to open the little doors of the stove and put on wood and coal. The house would get cold. Then, as the day went by, it would get darker. Even with all the lights turned on, it would still be dark outside.

When Grandpa was there, the stove
burned bright, and the sounds which came
from outside didn't matter. But what if she
and Scooter were alone, and strange
animals without names came down from
the moor to prowl around the house?

All at once, Alice decided what she
would do. If Grandpa and Mrs Hammond
didn't come, she and Scooter would go to
the village.

They would make their way, through the snow, all the way down the lane, and she would hold Scooter's hand tightly, so that he wouldn't be afraid.

She knelt down, to tell him about the plan. "Scooter," she said — but he wasn't listening. He was lying on the rug, gazing at the flames behind the stove doors. His cheeks were bright red, and his eyes were dreamy.

"Scooter!" she said again; and this time he looked at her.

"I'm hungry again," he said.

Alice sighed and got up, and made him some more bread and honey. Scooter sat by the window to eat. Alice looked at him, and wondered if he would be strong enough to make the long walk down the lane, or if he would get tired half way. She wondered if she would be strong enough to carry him.

"We'll have to try," she said to herself. "If no one comes, we'll both have to try, as hard as we can."

She got up from the rug, to go to him, to make him understand how serious everything was. But at that very moment, he knelt up suddenly on the window seat.

43

"It's stopped snowing!" he said. "I can see Grandpa! He's got the lamb!"

Alice ran to the window to look. Scooter was right — Grandpa was making his way across the moor; and over the top of the hedge Alice could see Mrs Hammond's red hat, bobbing along, as she made her way down the lane.

"When they get here," said Alice, "we'll tell them how good we've been. We'll tell them how we fed everyone. We'll say, 'everyone's had their breakfast!'"

She suddenly felt very happy and very proud of herself, and she tried to hug Scooter and kiss him, but he wouldn't let her. He began to run round the room, shouting, "Make the lamb some bread and honey! Make the lamb some bread and honey!"

"Don't be silly," said Alice, going back to the warm stove, and kneeling down on the rug. "Lambs don't eat bread and honey."

45

For a moment, she thought that Scooter was going to get angry again — but he didn't. He just stood behind her, and nuzzled his sticky face into the nape of her neck. Alice sat very still and quiet, and waited for the door to open, and for the lamb to come towards her, over the floor, on its long, black, wobbling legs.

PRINTED IN BELGIUM BY
proost
INTERNATIONAL BOOK PRODUCTION